Down on Casey's Farm

SANDRA JORDAN

ORCHARD BOOKS

New York

To my brother John Chris
Love you. . . .

Casey has a farm in his backyard, with an old wooden drawer for a barn.

Under the curving leaves
his pigs snort and snuffle.
The horses stamp their feet
in the dew-wet morning grass.
If you listen the way Casey does,
you might even hear a moo.

A calf wakes up in a dusky stall. Mama cow waits nearby.
Moo-o-o-o. It's time for breakfast.

Listen.
Do you hear a m-a-a?

Ma-a, ma-a, ma-a, get out of the way! A herd of hungry goats rushes through the gate with the baby kid in the lead.

Listen.
Do you hear a nibble, nibble, nibble?

The baby rabbits are out! They hop around the yard, looking for a way into the vegetable garden. Nibble, nibble, nibble. The weeds taste good, but have you seen a carrot or a cabbage?

Listen.
Do you hear a hum-m-m?

A mama llama hums to her baby cria
with the faint buzzy sound of a lazy bee.

Listen.
Do you hear a cheep, cheep, cheep?

Cheep, cheep, cheep, cheep, cheep. Five chicks scratch to find a juicy bug for lunch. Cluck, cluck, cluck, cluck, cluck. The mother hen fluffs up her feathers, and one by one the chicks creep underneath her wing for an afternoon nap.

Listen.
Do you hear an oink?

When the hot sun blazes,
the pigs cool off in squishy mud.
Oink, oink, oink, they say to the piglets.
Keep near the wallow. Don't go too far.

Listen. Do you hear a honk, honk, honk?

The Canada geese
swim proudly across the pond,
showing off their goslings.
Honk, honk, honk.
Paddle hard.
Follow me.
Stay in line.

Listen.
Do you hear a ba-a, ba-a, ba-a-a?

The shy lamb cuddles next to the thick winter coat of mama sheep. Ba-a, ba-a, ba-a-a.
The brave lamb explores a stream with his friend.

Listen.
Do you hear a meow?

Meow, meow.
By the toolshed door
mama cat feeds her kittens.
After dinner
they sit purring in the sun.

Listen. Do you hear a neigh?

Neigh, neigh, neigh.
The sun is setting.
Soon it will be dark.
The horse and her foal head
for the shelter of the barn.

Listen.
Do you hear a call?

Ca-a-a-sey!
Come inside—
your dinner's getting cold.

After dinner,
bath, and many stories,
Casey and the animals go to bed.

Listen. Do you hear a sh-h-h?

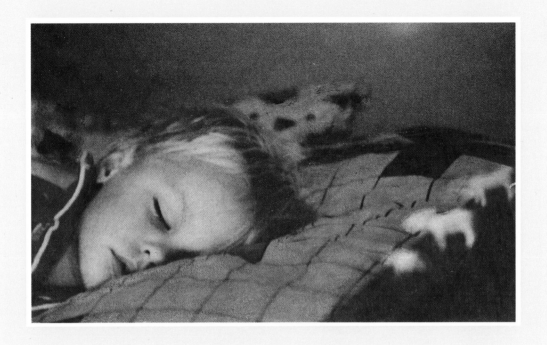

Sh-h-h.
It's time to snuggle into sleep,
and in the shadowed room
dream sweet animal dreams
of a new day on Casey's farm.

Good-night.

ORCHARD BOOKS • 95 Madison Avenue • New York, NY 10016

Library of Congress Cataloging-in-Publication Data   Jordan, Sandra, date.
Down on Casey's farm / Sandra Jordan.   p.   cm.
Summary: As Casey plays with his toy farm animals, he imagines their actions and sounds in his mind.   ISBN 0-531-09503-7.—ISBN 0-531-08853-7 (lib. bdg.)
[1. Domestic animals—Fiction.   2. Animal sounds—Fiction.]
I. Title.   PZ7.J7683Do   1996   [E]—dc20   95-41171

Printed by Barton Press, Inc. • Bound by Horowitz/Rae
BOOK DESIGN BY THE ANTLER & BALDWIN DESIGN GROUP

10 9 8 7 6 5 4 3 2 1

The text of this book is set in 16½ point ITC Berkeley Old Style.
The illustrations are hand-colored, sepia-toned photographs.
Manufactured in the United States of America

For six months I visited farms in Westport, Massachusetts, Tiverton and Little Compton, Rhode Island, northern New Jersey, Upstate New York, Boulder and Golden, Colorado, and northern Ohio, often pulling into the driveway without an introduction because I had spied a photogenic animal in a field. I want to thank all of the many farmers who generously let me wander around their farms with my cameras and took time from their busy schedules to show off a prize calf, chase baby rabbits around the garden, or call the goats in from the pasture to greet an unexpected visitor. The friends and family who scouted for animals and, as often as I could manage it, were dragooned into acting as unofficial photo assistants and good company include G. J. Askins, Ann Beneduce, Kathryn Bondi, Barbara Brodlieb, Toni and Roy DeMeo, Jan Greenberg, Nancie Jordan, Samantha Jordan, Max Weisberg, and of course my brother John Christopher Jordan, his wife Patti, and the children, his, hers, and theirs, most particularly Jack aka Casey. And last but surely most important to an idea becoming a book are Sallie Baldwin who designs, Neal Porter who edits, encourages, and cajoles as needed, and the other wonderful people at Orchard Books who care about every detail and nag so gently you hardly know it's happening. You know who you are.